my LiTTLE
PONY

This book
belongs to:

my Little
pony

ORCHARD BOOKS

First published in Great Britain in 2017 by The Watts Publishing Group

1 3 5 7 9 10 8 6 4 2



Written by Sarah Levison

Interior pages designed by Claire Yeo

A CIP catalogue record for this book is available from the British Library

ISBN 978 1 40835 153 6

Printed and bound in China

FSC www.fsc.org MIX Paper from responsible sources FSC® C104740

Orchard Books
An imprint of Hachette Children's Group
Part of The Watts Publishing Group Limited
Carmelite House
50 Victoria Embankment
London EC4Y 0DZ

An Hachette UK Company
www.hachette.co.uk

www.hachettechildrens.co.uk

Adult supervision is recommended for all baking and cooking activities, and when glue, paint, scissors and other sharp points are in use.

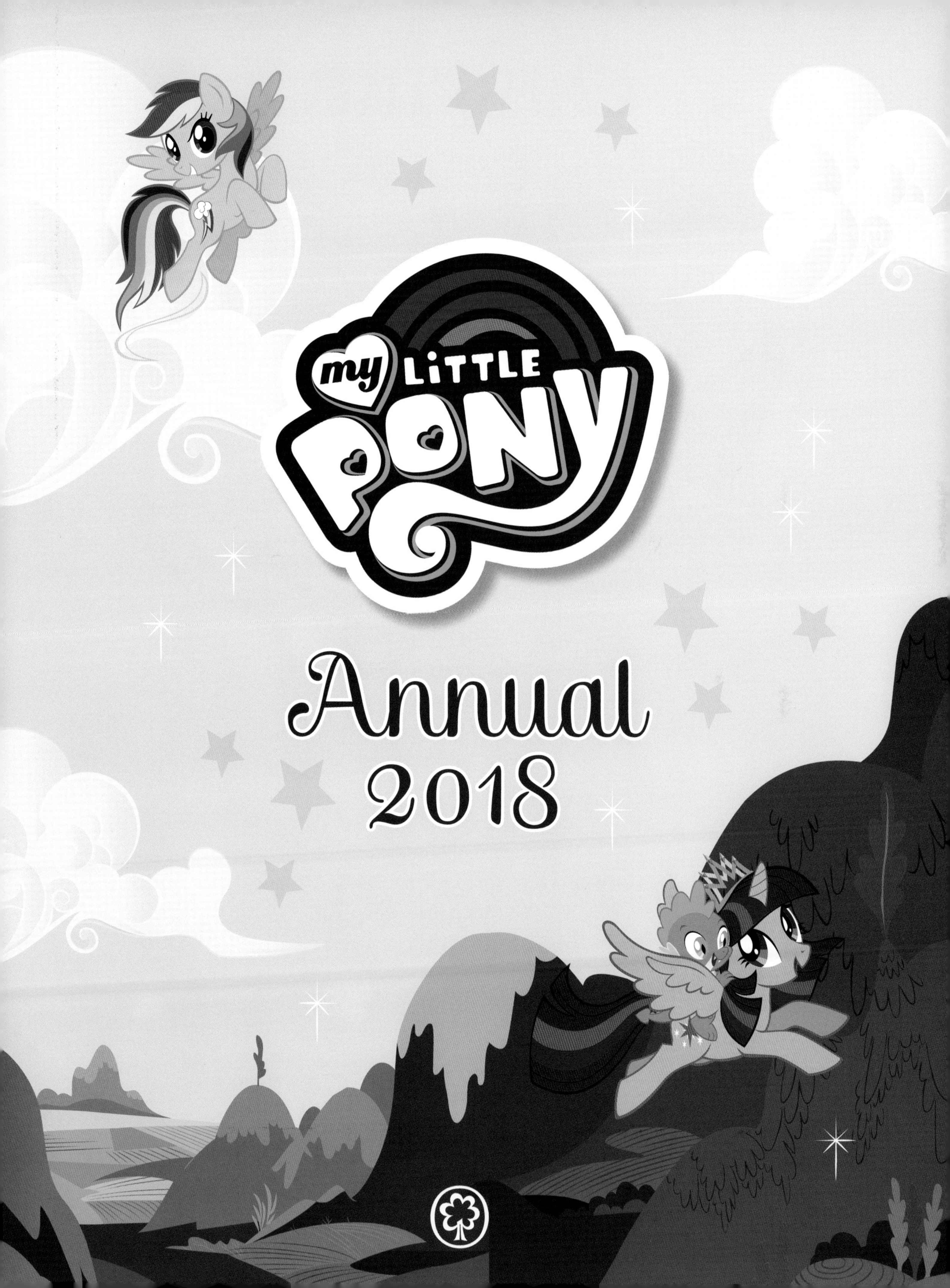
my LITTLE PONY
Annual
2018

# Contents

# Welcome!

Hey there, pony pal –
welcome to our ALL NEW annual!

We've had SO much fun filling this book with activities, stories, games, puzzles and more – it's EPIC! And there's a super special secret section all about our very own MOVIE. We're so excited to share our big screen adventures with you!

Big hugs, friendship flutters
and hoof bumps,

Princess Twilight Sparkle, Rainbow Dash,
Rarity, Fluttershy, Pinkie Pie,
Applejack and Spike

XOXOXO

# In the Know

There are always so many things going on in the magical world of My Little Pony! Here's a quick recap of what – and who – you need to know …

## AT THE BEGINNING …

Princess Celestia and her younger sister, Princess Luna, ruled the kingdom of Equestria together. Princess Celestia looked after daytime and Princess Luna ruled the night. But when Luna became jealous of Celestia, she turned into wicked Nightmare Moon.

## FRIENDSHIP IS MAGIC!

Princess Celestia sent Twilight Sparkle and Spike to Ponyville and here they met some very special friends – Pinkie Pie, Rarity, Applejack, Fluttershy and Rainbow Dash. Together, harnessing the power of friendship, the six ponies bravely destroyed Nightmare Moon. Princess Luna ruled alongside Princess Celestia once more, and peace returned to the kingdom.

## THE WONDERFUL WORLD OF EQUESTRIA

Equestria is a very special place, home to lots of magical creatures, like dragons, bears, griffons, sea serpents and more! The kingdom has icy mountains, deserts, forests, lakes and oceans. It's a truly wonderful world.

# Meet the Ponies

### PRINCESS TWILIGHT SPARKLE

**Home:** The Castle of Friendship
**Type of pony:** Alicorn
**Personality:** Patient, kind, a natural leader
**Loves:** Learning, books, magic

### RAINBOW DASH

**Home:** The Cloudominium
**Type of pony:** Pegasus
**Personality:** Confident, funny, loyal
**Loves:** Flying FAST, competitions, adventures

### PINKIE PIE

**Home:** Sugarcube Corner
**Type of pony:** Earth pony
**Personality:** Playful, funny, silly
**Loves:** Throwing parties, playing games, eating cupcakes

### FLUTTERSHY

**Home:** A cottage by Everfree Forest
**Type of pony:** Pegasus
**Personality:** Shy, kind, gentle
**Loves:** Animals, peace and quiet, tea parties

### APPLEJACK

**Home:** Sweet Apple Acres
**Type of pony:** Earth pony
**Personality:** Reliable, honest, hardworking
**Loves:** Being outdoors, her family, the farm

### RARITY

**Home:** The Carousel Boutique
**Type of pony:** Unicorn
**Personality:** Glamorous, generous, wise
**Loves:** Creating fabulous fashions, treating herself and her best friends

# Hopes and Dreams

Twilight Sparkle and her pony friends have many hopes and dreams – and those dreams are starting to come true. Rainbow Dash finally joined the Wonderbolts and Rarity has opened her boutique in Canterlot. Here are some words of wisdom from your pony pals about how to make YOUR dreams come true!

## FOLLOW YOUR HEART

Think about what truly makes you happy. Do you love spending time with animals? Or reading a good book? Use the things that you really love as a starting point. Twilight Sparkle loves to read and learn. She realised that she wanted to share her love of learning with others. Now she teaches valuable friendship lessons to Starlight Glimmer!

## WORK HARD

Rarity is a very talented designer and has a super-chic fashion boutique in Ponyville. But she had always dreamed of opening a magnificent store in Canterlot … and finally this dream became a reality. But talent alone wasn't enough! Rarity had to work hard to make sure the boutique was a success. Dreams stay as dreams unless you make them come true!

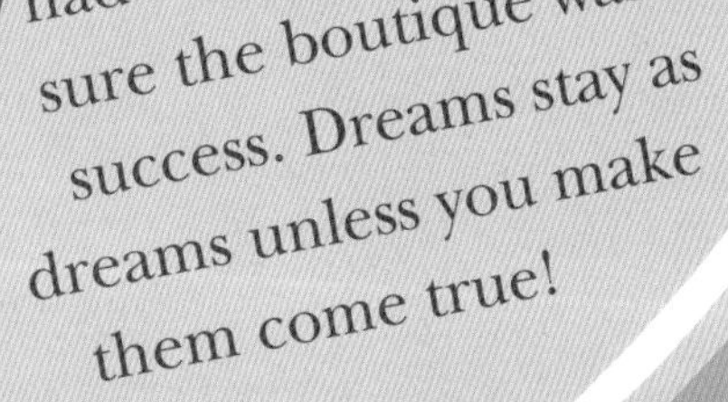

## LISTEN TO YOUR FRIENDS

Sometimes your friends know you better than you know yourself! When Applejack was worn out from all her farm chores, Rarity helped her to see that she needed a break. After a bit of time away from Sweet Apple Acres, Applejack felt much more like herself again!

## DON'T GIVE UP

Rainbow Dash had always dreamed about being in the Wonderbolts – flying fast and performing aerial acrobatics! But it took a long time for her to be accepted as part of the Wonderbolts team. This perky pony didn't give up and was eventually rewarded for her positive attitude. Rainbow Dash was born to soar!

## USE YOUR UNIQUE TALENT

Kind Fluttershy is always on hand to help her friends! She has modelled clothes for Rarity, lent her singing voice to Big McIntosh and often helps Pinkie Pie in the Sugarcube Bakery. But Fluttershy always knew that fulfilling her destiny would be connected to her love of animals. And this led to her opening up her very own animal sanctuary!

## TAKE TIME TO THINK

Pinkie Pie has SO much energy that she can't help but bounce, roll, gallop and leap into everything she tries! But sometimes we all need to stop and give ourselves time to think.

## DON'T BE A STRESSHEAD

The Cutie Mark Crusaders were SO desperate to discover their destiny and get their cutie marks that they tried to be good at everything! When they finally realised they just needed to relax, be themselves and help others, their cutie marks appeared. True cutie mark magic!

# WONDERBOLTS WORDSEARCH

Whoop, whoop! I'm Rainbow Dash and I'm the newest member of the Wonderbolts. Can you help me find all the names of my new team mates in the grid below? Tip: look backwards and diagonally too!

**Misty Fly**
**Blaze**
**Soarin**
**High Winds**
**Spitfire**
**Fleetfoot**

| k | a | y | l | f | y | t | s | i | m |
|---|---|---|---|---|---|---|---|---|---|
| z | b | l | x | t | w | l | l | y | s |
| e | k | l | p | w | u | t | i | w | s |
| i | l | s | a | p | p | o | n | x | p |
| t | g | y | y | z | l | w | l | u | i |
| r | v | l | z | l | e | s | k | r | t |
| l | j | w | q | w | a | s | y | s | f |
| f | l | e | e | t | f | o | o | t | i |
| u | e | s | i | h | q | a | r | h | r |
| s | i | p | q | e | j | r | n | k | e |
| a | z | y | l | k | c | i | m | v | z |
| h | i | g | h | w | i | n | d | s | o |

Answers on page 62.

# TOP TEAM

Use your colouring pens and pencils to bring this picture of Rainbow Dash to life!

# THE CUTIE MAP

**TWILIGHT SPARKLE AND HER FRIENDS** WERE IN THE **CASTLE OF FRIENDSHIP** WHEN A **MAGICAL MAP OF EQUESTRIA** APPEARED BEFORE THEM. THE PONIES' CUTIE MARKS SHONE ABOVE ONE SPOT ON THE MAP. **TWILIGHT SPARKLE** WAS SURE THAT SOMEONE THERE NEEDED SOME HELP.

THE FRIENDS TRAVELLED A LONG WAY ACROSS **EQUESTRIA** AND EVENTUALLY CAME TO A SMALL VILLAGE. THE PONIES WHO LIVED THERE LOOKED VERY HAPPY. BUT THE FRIENDS WERE PUZZLED: THESE PONIES ALL HAD **EXACTLY THE SAME CUTIE MARK**, A "=" SIGN. PINKIE PIE WAS **SUSPICIOUS** OF THE PONIES' IDENTICAL SMILES!

**THE FRIENDS DECIDED TO FIND OUT MORE ...**

THE FRIENDS WENT TO SEE THE VILLAGE LEADER, **STARLIGHT GLIMMER**. "WE'RE ALWAYS HAPPY TO WELCOME PONIES WHO WANT TO EXPERIENCE TRUE FRIENDSHIP FOR THE FIRST TIME!" GUSHED THE SUPER-FRIENDLY PONY. SHE EXPLAINED WHY THE PONIES IN THE VILLAGE HAD THE SAME CUTIE MARK: **THEY LOVED BEING EXACTLY THE SAME!** THEY DIDN'T NEED TO HAVE UNIQUE TALENTS.

**STARLIGHT GLIMMER** EXPLAINED THAT THE VILLAGE PONIES NEVER DISAGREED ABOUT ANYTHING. "EACH OF US WAS ONCE BLINDED BY THE FALSE PROMISE OF OUR CUTIE MARKS," SHE SAID. **BUT SOMETHING STILL DIDN'T SEEM QUITE RIGHT TO THE FRIENDS** ...

A PONY NAMED **SUGAR BELLE** DIDN'T UNDERSTAND HOW THE SIX PONIES COULD DISAGREE ON SOME THINGS BUT STILL STAY FRIENDS! **RARITY** EXPLAINED THAT IT WAS THE DIFFERENCES IN THEIR PERSONALITIES THAT MADE THE SIX FRIENDS GET ON SO WELL. **"MEET ME IN THE CELLAR BEFORE YOU GO,"** SUGAR BELLE WHISPERED.

**SUGAR BELLE** EXPLAINED THAT **STARLIGHT GLIMMER** HAD TAKEN THE VILLAGE PONIES' CUTIE MARKS IN A **SPECIAL CEREMONY**. THE CUTIE MARKS WERE KEPT IN A CUTIE MARK VAULT. TWILIGHT SPARKLE DECIDED THAT THE MAGICAL MAP MUST HAVE LED THEM TO THE VILLAGE TO HELP RETURN THE PONIES' UNIQUE CUTIE MARKS! **THE FRIENDS KNEW THEY HAD TO VISIT THE VAULT.**

STARLIGHT GLIMMER USED A **MAGICAL STAFF** TO REMOVE THE SIX FRIENDS' CUTIE MARKS AND REPLACE THEM WITH THE SAME "=" MARK AS EVERYONE ELSE! **"WE'LL SHOW YOU JUST HOW MUCH BETTER LIFE CAN BE WITHOUT YOUR CUTIE MARKS!"** SHE CRIED.

STARLIGHT GLIMMER LOCKED THE SIX PONY PALS IN A ROOM. EACH PONY HAD LOST THE SPECIAL SKILLS THAT MADE HER **UNIQUE**! FLUTTERSHY WAS SAD THAT SHE COULDN'T COMMUNICATE WITH A LITTLE BIRD THAT CAME TO THE WINDOW. **TWILIGHT SPARKLE CAME UP WITH A PLAN:** IF FRIENDLY **FLUTTERSHY** PRETENDED SHE WAS HAPPY TO LIVE IN THE VILLAGE, THEN SHE WOULD BE FREED.

THE PLAN WORKED AND FLUTTERSHY WAS FREED. THAT NIGHT, SHE DISCOVERED THAT THE SIX CUTIE MARKS WERE AT **STARLIGHT GLIMMER'S** HOUSE. STARLIGHT WANTED TO KEEP THEM CLOSE TO HER, AND WAS PARTICULARLY INTERESTED IN **TWILIGHT SPARKLE'S CUTIE MARK** ...

AND THAT WASN'T ALL ... THAT MORNING, **FLUTTERSHY** LEARNED THAT **STARLIGHT** STILL HAD HER UNIQUE CUTIE MARK! FLUTTERSHY REVEALED THIS CUTIE MARK AND FREED HER FRIENDS. THE VILLAGE PONIES WERE VERY UPSET. STARLIGHT GLIMMER TRIED TO PERSUADE THE PONIES THAT SHE HAD KEPT HER OWN CUTIE MARK FOR THE GOOD OF EVERYONE, BUT THE VILLAGERS TURNED AGAINST HER!

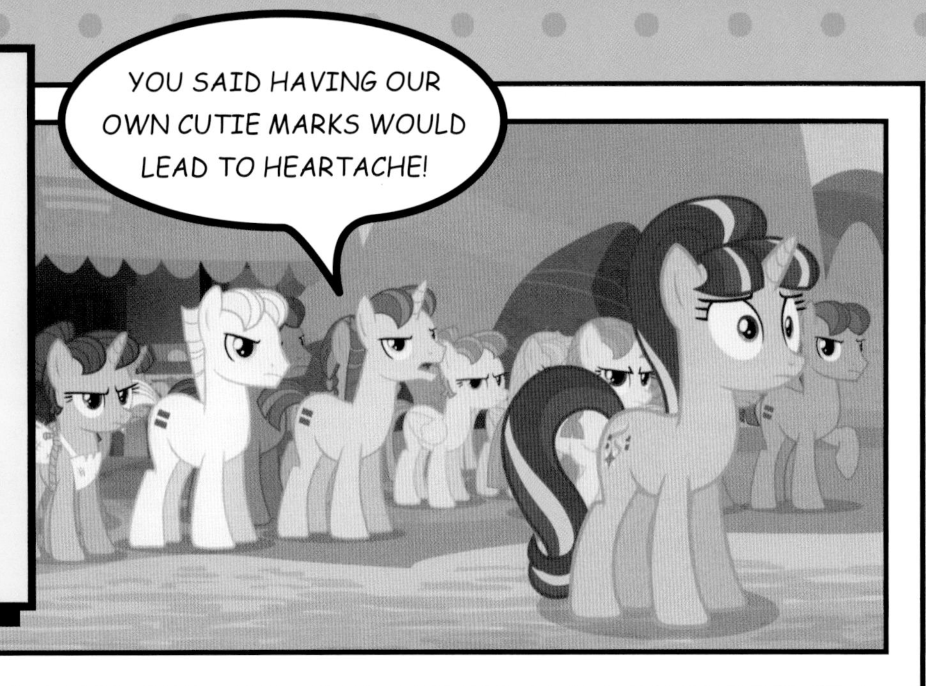

YOU SAID HAVING OUR OWN CUTIE MARKS WOULD LEAD TO HEARTACHE!

THE VILLAGERS COLLECTED THEIR CUTIE MARKS FROM THE VAULT. STARLIGHT ESCAPED WITH THE **CUTIE MARKS BELONGING TO TWILIGHT SPARKLE AND HER FRIENDS**. BUT THE VILLAGERS CHASED STARLIGHT AND FREED THE CUTIE MARKS! TWILIGHT SPARKLE TRIED TO REASON WITH THE MEAN PONY. **"EACH OF MY FRIENDS HAS TAUGHT ME SOMETHING DIFFERENT ABOUT MYSELF,"** SHE EXPLAINED. BUT STARLIGHT GLIMMER USED HER MAGIC TO DISAPPEAR INTO THE MOUNTAINS.

THE HAPPY VILLAGERS DECIDED TO STAY IN THE VILLAGE, BUT NOW THEY WOULD REJOICE IN THE UNIQUE MAGIC OF THEIR CUTIE MARKS AND CELEBRATE THEIR DIFFERENCES! **"THE MAP DID HAVE A REASON FOR SENDING US HERE,"** SAID **APPLEJACK.** THE BEST FRIENDS DECIDED TO JOIN THE VILLAGE PARTY BEFORE THEY HEADED BACK TO PONYVILLE. WHO KNEW WHERE THE NEXT ADVENTURE WOULD TAKE THEM!

WE'VE BROUGHT REAL FRIENDSHIP TO THESE PONIES!

**THE END**

# All About … STARLIGHT GLIMMER!

Starlight Glimmer did not make a good first impression on the ponies – taking cutie marks from the village ponies and being sneaky and dishonest. But Princess Twilight Sparkle believes in the magic of friendship … and that everyone deserves a second chance – even Starlight Glimmer!

## APPEARANCE

Starlight Glimmer is a unicorn, like Rarity. She has a lavender coat and a purple mane with teal streaks running through it. Her purple eyes flash wildly when she is angry!

## CUTIE MARK

Starlight's real cutie mark is a purple and white star and two glimmering blue streams.

## MAGIC

Starlight Glimmer has powerful magical abilities. She can create magical barriers, distracting lights, and shoot powerful blasts of magic!

## TRUE FRIENDS

When the ponies first met Starlight Glimmer, it seemed she had lots of friends in the village. But Starlight showed that she was not a true friend. Twilight Sparkle hoped that one day Starlight would understand the true happiness that friendship can bring.

## MYSTERIOUS PAST

Nobody knows where Starlight came from but over time more is sure to be revealed about this powerful pony …

# Starlight's Magical Mix-up

Oh no! Starlight Glimmer has used her powerful magic to mix up this image of the Mane Six! Can you use your special pony pal powers to complete this picture? Use the picture at the top of the page as a guide.

# Royal Recap

Hi there, friends! It's Twilight Sparkle here. I'm so proud to be part of the Equestria royal family. We all work together to look after this wonderful kingdom and everypony who lives here. But I haven't always been a princess! Princess Celestia made me "Princess of Friendship" for my dedication to learning about magic and friendship.

**Here's all you need to know about your royal friends …**

## DID YOU KNOW?

I live in the Castle of Friendship with Spike. This castle appeared after my original home, the Golden Oak Library, was destroyed in a fierce battle with Lord Tirek.

## DID YOU KNOW?

When Princess Celestia performs magic, her mane and tail glow different colours!

## PRINCESS CELESTIA

rules Equestria, alongside her sister, Princess Luna. She uses her magic to make the sun rise each morning and set each night, and maintains harmony throughout the kingdom. Princess Celestia acts as a mentor to me, sharing her knowledge and wisdom.

## PRINCESS LUNA

is Celestia's younger sister and looks up to her for guidance and advice. Princess Luna transformed into Nightmare Moon for many years, and was banished from the kingdom. Thankfully, those days are over and now she cares for Equestria as much as her sister.

## DID YOU KNOW?

Princess Cadance's official name is Princess Mi Amore Cadenza. Fancy!

## PRINCESS CADANCE

used to foalsit for me when I was little, and we are firm friends! Cadance rules the Crystal Empire alongside Prince Shining Armor. Cadance is kind and caring and makes sure the ponies of the sparkling Crystal Empire are happy.

## PRINCESS FLURRY HEART

is Cadance and Shining Armor's adorable foal! This tiny princess was the first alicorn ever to be born in Equestria. This means that her magic is very powerful. She could fly as fast as Rainbow Dash when she was just a few days old and her sneeze creates a powerful blast of magic!

## DID YOU KNOW?

Flurry Heart was given her name after a special "crystalling" ceremony.

## DID YOU KNOW?

Princess Luna can control the weather! She's particularly skilled at using lightning and creating a thick mist.

## SHINING ARMOR

became Prince Shining Armor when he married Princess Cadance. This unicorn is head of the royal guard and defends the Crystal Empire against fearsome foes such as King Sombra. He is also my big brother!

## DID YOU KNOW?

Shining Armor was so happy when I had my official coronation that he shed a few tears of "liquid pride". Aww!

# Marvellous Mini Crowns!

## YOU WILL NEED:

Empty kitchen roll tubes, cut in half

Scissors

Fabric glue

PVA glue

Thin elastic cord or a length of string

## DECORATIONS:

Some or all of the following:

Several sheets of brightly coloured felt

Loose glitter

Stick-on jewels

Mini pompoms

Wrapping paper

Foil

Colouring pens and pencils

Stickers

Paints

Each of the pony princesses has their own unique crown or tiara and now you can have one too! Here is Rarity's guide to making the perfect royal headwear.

1. Cut out a piece of brightly coloured felt the same height as your cardboard tube. The piece should be wide enough to fit neatly around the tube. Suggested dimensions: 10.5 cm height and 16.5 cm width.

2. Cover one side of the felt with fabric glue. Wrap this around your tube. You may need help from a grown-up for this part – it's a bit sticky!

**3**

Put the cardboard tube aside for half an hour or until the glue has dried.

**4**

Now it's time to create your crown! Ask a grown-up for help with this stage. Using your scissors, carefully cut out triangle shapes from the tube. These should be approximately 3 cm deep and there should be four in total.

**5**

Ask a grown-up to make two small holes on opposite sides at the bottom of your crown. Then thread a length of elastic (or string) through these holes and tie two knots to fix it in place. The elastic needs to be the right length to sit under your chin with the crown on your head.

**6**

Now you can begin to decorate your crown. Why not stick pompoms around the base, and jewels to the peaks of the crown!

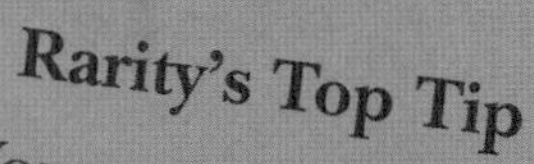

**Rarity's Top Tip**

You can make your crown tall or short – try some different versions and see which you like best!

## CUSTOMISE YOUR CROWN BY TRYING OUT THESE DIFFERENT DESIGNS:

**GORGEOUS GLITTER:** Go straight to step 4, making the "tips" of your crown. Cover the outside of the cardboard tube with PVA glue. Tip glitter on to a piece of paper and roll the crown in the glitter. Leave to dry. Don't forget to tip the leftover glitter back into the pot!

**FANTASTIC WRAPPING:** Instead of using felt in step 1, cover your tube with colourful wrapping paper. Once the glue is dry, decorate the crown.

**PRETTY PAINTS:** Skip steps 1–3 and instead paint your crown in your favourite colours. When the paint has dried, move on to steps 4–6.

# All About ... YOU!

Your pony friends want to find out all about YOU! Use a pen or pencil to fill in these pages and don't forget to add pictures!

My name is: ........................................................

My nickname is: ..............................................

Here's what I look like:

My age is: ..............................

The date of my birthday is:

..................................................

My star sign is: ..................

Draw a picture of yourself or stick a photo into this space!

My best friends' names are: ....................................,

.................................., ................................. .

The dates of my best friends' birthdays are:

.................., ...................., ..................... .

Draw a picture of your family or stick a photo into this space!

My family look like this:

THESE ARE SOME OF MY FAVOURITE THINGS:

MY LITTLE PONY ..............................

BOOK ..............................

ANIMAL ..............................

SPORT ..............................

FRUIT ..............................

TV PROGRAMME ..............................

ICE-CREAM FLAVOUR ..............................

CLOTHING ..............................

HOBBY ..............................

GAME ..............................

SCHOOL SUBJECT ..............................

TEACHER ..............................

# EYES ON THE PRIZE

Well, howdy-doo, pony partners! It's your friend Applejack here. Boy, have I got a challenge for you. Look at this first picture of my family reunion, then look at picture number two ...

1

There are EIGHT differences between the pictures, but y'all need to have your wits about you to spot them!
If you manage to spot all eight, then YEE-HAH! You're an awesome pony spotter.
2

Answers on page 62.

# Family Fun for Everyone

There are so many friendly ponies in Equestria, but how much do you know about the families of your favourite ponies? Test your knowledge by answering the questions below!

1

RARITY HAS A LITTLE SISTER CALLED ...

A SCOOTALOO
B SWEETIE BELLE
C SPIKE
D APPLE BLOOM

2

TWILIGHT SPARKLE'S BROTHER IS MARRIED TO WHICH OF THESE PONIES?

A PRINCESS CELESTIA
B PRINCESS LUNA
C PRINCESS CADANCE
D PRINCESS EMBER

3

APPLEJACK HAS A VERY LARGE FAMILY! WHAT IS THE NAME OF HER BROTHER?

A BIG HEAD
B BIG MACARONI
C BIG STEVE
D BIG MCINTOSH

Answers on page 62.

4

PINKIE PIE JUST ADORES LIVING IN PONYVILLE! BUT WHERE DID THIS PARTY PONY LIVE WHEN SHE WAS YOUNGER?

A ON A ROCK FARM
B ON A STRAWBERRY FARM
C IN A CUPCAKE FACTORY
D IN AN ORCHARD

5

FLUTTERSHY LOVES HER ANIMAL FRIENDS SO MUCH SHE THINKS OF THEM AS HER FAMILY! WHAT IS THE NAME OF FLUTTERSHY'S SPECIAL ANIMAL FRIEND?

A ANGIE
B ANGEL
C PETAL
D FLUFFY

6

THE NAMES OF MR AND MRS CAKE'S ENERGETIC TWIN TODDLERS ARE ...

A PLUM CAKE AND PUMPERNICKEL
B POUND CAKE AND PUMPKIN CAKE
C SPONGE CAKE AND CUPCAKE
D MARZIPAN AND MERINGUE

7

WHICH CUTIE MARK CRUSADER IDOLISES RAINBOW DASH AND WISHES SHE WAS HER BIG SISTER?

A SCOOTALOO
B APPLE BLOOM
C BABS SEED
D SWEETIE BELLE

8

WHAT IS THE NAME OF PRINCESS CELESTIA'S DISTANT NEPHEW?

A PRINCE BLUEBEARD
B PRINCE BLUEBOTTLE
C PRINCE BLUEBLOOD
D PRINCE FANCYPANTS

# CUTIE MARK CRAZINESS

Can you finish filling in the grid below by drawing in the correct cutie marks? Each cutie mark should appear once in each row, column and 4x4 square.

Answer on page 62.

Oh. My. I am super-duper, over-the-moon, hold-on-to-your-hooves EXCITED to be starring in a MOVIE with my very best friends! It really is our most AWESOME ADVENTURE yet. Turn the page for my lowdown on the showdown …

# Our Greatest Adventure Yet

Princess Twilight Sparkle was organizing the Friendship Festival and she was **SUPER** stressed as ponies were arriving from all over Equestria and there was so much to do!

In the throne room of Canterlot Castle, Twilight presented her plans for the festival to Celestia, Luna and Cadance. The highlight? A spectacular **light show**, powered by the princesses' magic!

BUT – oh no! – the princesses refused to lend Twilight their powers. She already had all the magic she needed, they told her – the magic of **FRIENDSHIP**!

The rest of us agreed – and I gave Twilight a bit of a pep talk. Then all six of us got straight to work …

Rainbow Dash cleared the clouds while Applejack handed out free samples of delicious apple juice from her cart.

Fluttershy and her bird chorus got busy rehearsing some super special songs (with help from Angel Bunny!).

And Twilight needn't have worried about the festival not having enough sparkle – Rarity was putting jewels on **EVERYTHING**! Almost as impressive as my balloon decorations (recognise anyone?!).

Twilight Sparkle was starting to feel better – well, until my new party cannon fired cake frosting over megastar singer Songbird Serenade ... **Ooopsie!**

But if we thought things were getting **STICKY**, we hadn't seen anything yet. We were about to embark on the adventure of a lifetime – one that would take us far beyond Equestria ...

# Meet the Movie Stars!

There are lots of new friends – and foes! – to meet in *My Little Pony: The Movie.* Here's a guide to who's who!

## THE STORM KING

This terrifying creature can harness thunder and create terrifying tornadoes. He won't let anypony stand in his way … but he hasn't yet come up against the powerful magic of friendship. Watch out, Storm King!

## TEMPEST

This mysterious unicorn obeys the orders of the Storm King. She has a broken horn and a very bad temper!

## STORM CREATURES

These mean fiends do whatever the Storm King tells them to.

## GRUBBER

This greedy creature is Tempest's sidekick. He's a bit of a chatterbox and he loves to eat lots of cake.

## CAPTAIN CELAENO

Brave Captain Celaeno uses her swashbuckling skills to lead a crew of parrot pirates. This feathered bunch are the friendliest pirates you're ever likely to meet!

## CAPPER

Capper is the coolest cat in town and he seems to be a good friend to the ponies … But can they *really* trust him?

The Storm King has sent Tempest on an important mission. But where is her greedy sidekick, Grubber? Help Tempest through the maze to find him!

Answers on page 62.

# AHOY THERE, PIRATE PALS!

Ooh arr, me hearties, it's Twilight Sparkle here! In *My Little Pony: The Movie*, my friends and I have an incredible adventure on a pirate ship. Can you match each of our new pirate pals with the right name and description? Draw a line to connect them.

1

2

3

4

**FACT**

**Pirate LixSpittle** carries cutlery in his pocket.

**FACT**

**Captain Celaeno** wears a large feather in her hat.

**FACT**

**Pirate Murdoch** always wears flying goggles.

**FACT**

**Pirate Boyle** has just one hand.

Answers on page 62.

# Pirate Ponies to the Rescue

Shiver me timbers! Look carefully at these pictures of the ponies in their pirate gear. Can you spot the twelve differences between the two pictures? Write down what they are when you've spotted them!

Answers on page 62.

1:
2:
3:
4:
5:
6:
7:
8:
9:
10:
11:
12:

# Seapony Magic

Join the ponies as they explore a wonderful underwater world of fun and friendship! Here's your special guide to all their new undersea friends!

## QUEEN NOVO

This beautiful creature is the wise and kind ruler of the seaponies. She lives with her daughter, Princess Skystar, in a breathtaking undersea castle.

## PRINCESS SKYSTAR

This plucky princess is Queen Novo's daughter. She is so pleased when Pinkie Pie and friends come to visit – she's lonely in the castle! The princess is very kind and looks after all the sea creatures and fish.

## AMAZING CREATURES

The ponies are amazed by the extraordinary creatures they meet in the ocean, from brightly coloured fish, to shiny molluscs and vast glowing jellyfish!

## NEW FRIENDS

When Pinkie Pie and her friends throw a party to cheer up Princess Skystar, they make plenty of new friends – the seaponies all want to hear about life in far-off Equestria!

## PUFFER FISH FUN

Dragons aren't usually found underwater but Spike is the exception: he's turned into a spiky puffer fish! He can make himself bigger by sucking in water – Supersize Spike!

## TERRIFIC TRANSFORMATION!

The pony friends are delighted to be transformed into seaponies. Rainbow Dash has fun whizzing around at top speed. Pinkie Pie learns to perform amazing somersaults, and Fluttershy loves making friends with the sea creatures!

# Code Crackers

Can you reveal a special message using the code below? Look closely at the symbols and write the corresponding letters in the empty boxes.

Answers on page 62.

# Underwater I-Spy

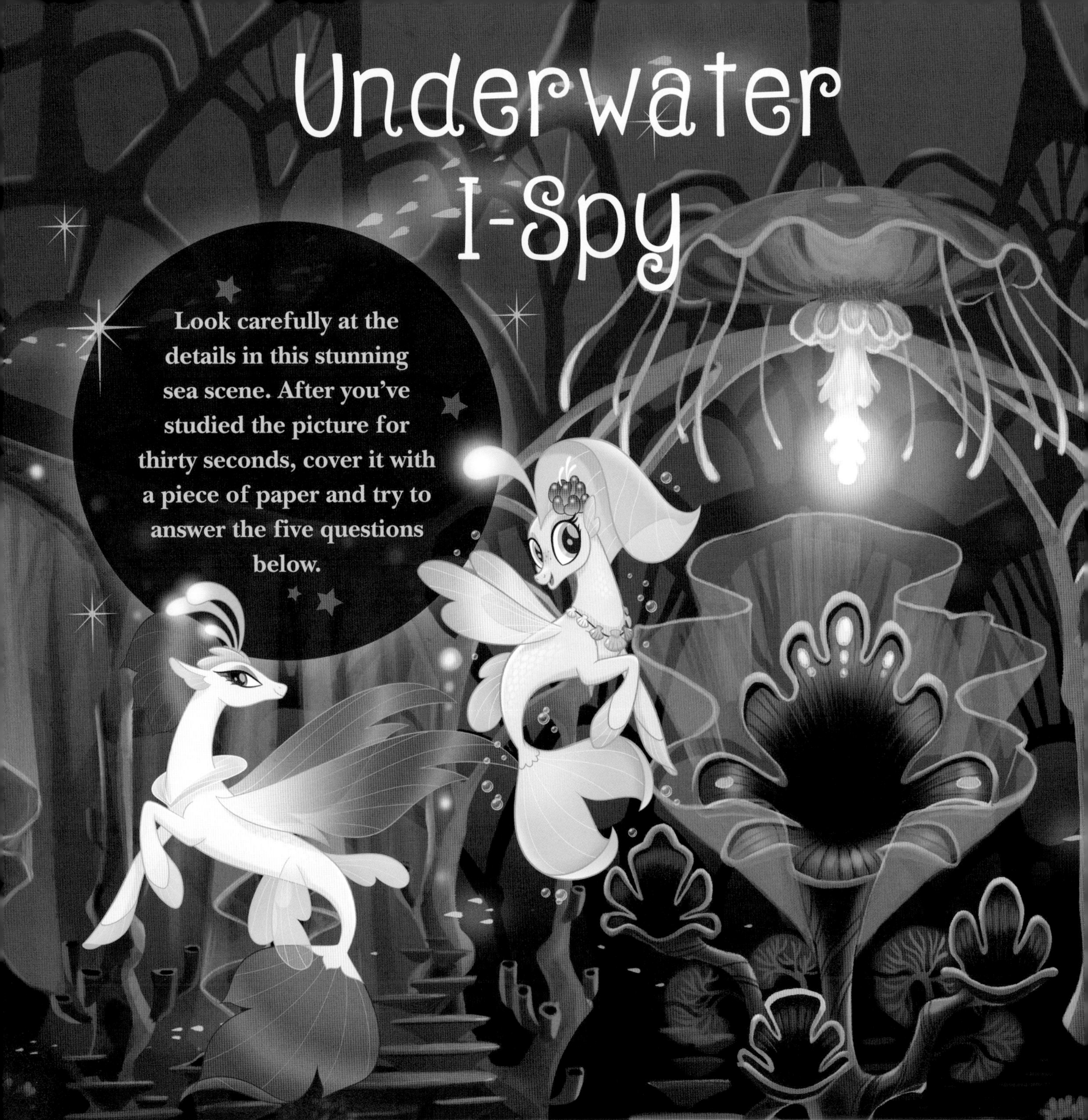

Look carefully at the details in this stunning sea scene. After you've studied the picture for thirty seconds, cover it with a piece of paper and try to answer the five questions below.

1: What glowing sea creature hangs above the throne?

2: What colour is Queen Novo's throne?

3: What decorates Princess Skystar's necklace?

4: Does Queen Novo have back legs or a beautiful tail?

5: What colour are the fish swimming through the throne room?

Answers on page 62.

# Adventure and Friendship Forever

Are you ready to play the *My Little Pony: The Movie* game, meeting new friends and foes along the way? Ask a friend or two to play with you!

1
START
2
3
4
You help Princess Twilight Sparkle prepare for the Friendship Festival.
MOVE FORWARDS TWO SPACES
5
6
7
Oh no! Tempest and Grubber block your way.
MISS A TURN
8
9
10
Songbird Serenade arrives to sing at the festival.
MOVE FORWARDS TWO SPACES
11
12
13
Grubber eats all your snacks.
GO BACK ONE SPACE
14
15
You and your friends meet Capper the Cat.
MOVE FORWARDS TWO SPACES

How to Play
★ You'll need a dice and at least one friend to play with.
★ Choose a button or a coin to use as your counter (or a small My Little Pony toy).
★ Throw the dice and then take it in turns to move around the board. The first one to reach the end is the winner!
30
You and your friends have succeeded in your mission.
YOU'RE A WINNER!
29
28
27
You come face to face with a horde of scary storm creatures!
MISS A TURN
20
Adventuring has made you tired.
MISS A TURN
19
21
18
You are helped by some pirate parrots.
MOVE FORWARDS ONE SPACE
22
You meet some friendly seaponies deep underwater.
GO FORWARDS FOUR SPACES
26
25
You encounter the terrifying Storm King.
GO BACK TWO SPACES
17
16
23
24

# Superstar

## Songbird Serenade!

Songbird Serenade is the coolest pop-pony in all of Equestria. Princess Twilight Sparkle has invited her to sing at the Friendship Festival. Colour in this picture and be sure to use your sparkliest pens and pencils!

# STORY TIME

**We've come to the end of the special My Little Pony movie section! Can you fill in the missing words to show what you know about the ponies' super-special friendship adventure?**

Twilight Sparkle was organising the first ever ____________ Festival! But she was super stressed as princesses Celestia, Luna and Cadance refused to lend her their ______ for an amazing light show.

Luckily her friends were happy to _____! Rarity decorated the Festival with beautiful _____. Applejack gave out _______ juice. Fluttershy and her _____ chorus prepared a special performance. Rainbow Dash cleared away all the _______ and Pinkie Pie made _________ decorations.

Everypony was excited when singer __________ Serenade arrived to perform the opening song ... but then Pinkie Pie's party cannon fired _____ frosting all over her. Oops, what a sticky start!

But things were about to get even stickier ... Would the ponies succeed in protecting ___________ from danger? One thing was for sure ... They were ready for the adventure!

Need some help? Select the missing words from this list. But beware – the words have become jumbled up and are not in the correct order!

apple gems Songbird magic
bird cake balloon clouds
help Friendship Equestria

Answers on page 62.

Wow! Pirates, seaponies, a superstar singer and a very mean Storm King … that's one CRAZY friendship adventure! Want to know the full story? Look out for our brilliant movie!
Can't wait till then? Here are a few of our favourite scenes …

my LITTLE PONY The MOVIE

# Guess Who?

How well do you know your My Little Pony pals? Read the clues carefully and then write the name of the correct character below the description.

## MYSTERY FRIEND ONE

I'm the latest member of the royal family.

I am an Alicorn.

I have big blue eyes.

..............................

## MYSTERY FRIEND TWO

**I love to fly FAST and HIGH.**

**I have a rainbow-coloured mane.**

**My cutie mark is a lightning bolt.**

..............................

## MYSTERY FRIEND THREE

I am NOT a pony!

I am best friends with Princess Twilight Sparkle.

I have magical green fire breath.

..............................

## MYSTERY FRIEND FOUR

I have a bright pink mane and tail.

I'm the bounciest pony in town.

I love to laugh and have fun.

..............................

Answers on page 62.

Chic Boutique
Opening up my very own boutique in Canterlot
is truly a dream come true. Can you help me
prepare my boutique for its grand opening?
It needs to be bursting with colour!

# Flutter Brutter

IT WAS LUNCHTIME IN CLOUDSDALE AND **FLUTTERSHY** WAS VISITING HER MUM AND DAD. **RAINBOW DASH** HAD COME ALONG TOO.

"IT'S SO NICE TO SEE YOU," FLUTTERSHY SMILED AT HER PARENTS.

SUDDENLY THE DOOR BURST OPEN AND IN CAME **ZEPHYR BREEZE**, FLUTTERSHY'S YOUNGER BROTHER.

ZEPHYR WAS THE **LAZIEST** PONY FLUTTERSHY KNEW – HE NEVER STUCK AT ONE THING FOR LONG! HE **ALWAYS** QUIT AS SOON AS THE GOING GOT TOUGH! "OH, NO!" FLUTTERSHY WHISPERED. IT LOOKED LIKE ZEPHYR WAS MOVING BACK IN WITH THEIR PARENTS!

IN NO TIME AT ALL, ZEPHYR HAD RUINED LUNCH, INSULTED RAINBOW DASH AND UPSET FLUTTERSHY! HE WOULDN'T ADMIT THAT HE'D ALREADY GIVEN UP ON HIS LATEST PLAN, TO BECOME A **SUCCESSFUL MANE STYLIST**.

"THEY JUST WEREN'T READY FOR MY AMAZING NEW IDEAS!" HE BOASTED. **"I NEEDED MY CREATIVE FREEDOM!"**

"I DON'T THINK LETTING ZEPHYR MOVE HOME IS A GOOD IDEA!" FLUTTERSHY WARNED HER MUM AND DAD.

HE'S VERY LAZY AND HE HAS TO LEARN TO STAND ON HIS OWN FOUR HOOVES!

BACK IN **PONYVILLE**, FLUTTERSHY WAS COMPLAINING ABOUT HER BROTHER TO **PINKIE PIE** AND **APPLEJACK**.

"I LOVE HIM BUT HE HAS NEVER LEARNT TO DO ANYTHING FOR HIMSELF!" SHE EXPLAINED.

"MAYBE YOU NEED TO STAND UP FOR YOUR PARENTS," SUGGESTED APPLEJACK. **"TEACH HIM THAT HE CAN'T TROT ALL OVER THEM!"**

FLUTTERSHY DECIDED THAT WAS WHAT SHE WAS GOING TO DO.

FLUTTERSHY FLEW STRAIGHT BACK UP TO CLOUDSDALE. "IT'S TIME FOR YOU TO STOP RELYING ON MUM AND DAD," SHE TOLD ZEPHYR FIRMLY. **"YOU HAVE TO BE MORE RESPECTFUL!"**

**HER BROTHER STORMED OUT.** THERE WERE PLENTY OF OTHER PLACES HE COULD GO, HE TOLD HER ...

... INCLUDING HER OWN HOUSE. YES, LATER THAT DAY, ZEPHYR TURNED UP AT **FLUTTERSHY'S COTTAGE**.

"YOU CAN STAY, BUT ONLY IF YOU GET A JOB," SHE INSISTED.

**"ABSOLUTELY, SIS!"** AGREED HER BROTHER.

FLUTTERSHY ARRANGED FOR ZEPHYR TO HELP **RARITY** IN THE **CAROUSEL BOUTIQUE**, STARTING THE VERY NEXT DAY.

BUT CARELESS ZEPHYR RUINED THE FABRIC RARITY HAD ASKED HIM TO DYE. RARITY WAS FURIOUS. **"YOUR BROTHER IS SO LAZY. HE CAN'T DO ANYTHING PROPERLY!"** SHE RAGED AT FLUTTERSHY.

ZEPHYR'S NEXT JOB WAS TO **CLEAN THE WINDOWS** IN **PRINCESS TWILIGHT SPARKLE**'S CASTLE OF FRIENDSHIP. BUT LAZY **ZEPHYR** PERSUADED **SPIKE** TO DO THE CLEANING.

**"YOU DIDN'T DO ANY WORK AT ALL!"** FUMED FLUTTERSHY.

"IT WAS JUST **TOO HARD**," ZEPHYR MOANED.

"YOU HAVE TO LEARN TO FINISH SOMETHING FOR ONCE!" SAID FLUTTERSHY. "YOU CAN'T CARRY ON LIVING WITH ME IF YOU'RE NOT GOING TO DO SOMETHING USEFUL. **YOU HAVE TO GO!"**

**RAINBOW DASH** TOLD FLUTTERSHY THAT SHE HAD DONE THE RIGHT THING. **"YOU COULDN'T LET ZEPHYR BEHAVE AS BADLY WITH YOU AS HE DOES WITH YOUR PARENTS!"** SHE EXPLAINED.

JUST THEN A FRIENDLY BIRD APPEARED AT THE WINDOW. ZEPHYR WAS HAVING A HORRIBLE TIME IN THE FOREST, SHE TOLD FLUTTERSHY. HE WANTED TO SEE HER.

**KIND-HEARTED** FLUTTERSHY WENT TO FIND HER BROTHER IMMEDIATELY. SOBBING, ZEPHYR EXPLAINED WHY HE ALWAYS GAVE UP ON EVERYTHING – BEING A MANE STYLIST, WORKING WITH RARITY, HELPING TWILIGHT SPARKLE – HE WAS AFRAID OF FAILING!

FLUTTERSHY FINALLY UNDERSTOOD. **"YOU HAVE TO GIVE THINGS A GO, EVEN IF YOU MIGHT FAIL,"** SHE SAID GENTLY. "IF NOT, YOU'LL NEVER LEARN ANYTHING!"

TOGETHER THEY RETURNED TO FLUTTERSHY'S COTTAGE. ZEPHYR DECIDED THAT HE WANTED TO FINISH HIS TRAINING TO BE A MANE STYLIST. **"I KNOW YOU CAN DO IT!"** FLUTTERSHY TOLD HIM.

"I'LL GIVE IT MY VERY BEST SHOT," SAID ZEPHYR.

JUST A FEW WEEKS LATER **ZEPHYR GRADUATED FROM HIS MANE STYLING CLASS!** "I'M SO PROUD OF YOU," SAID FLUTTERSHY.

MR AND MRS SHY WERE DELIGHTED. ZEPHYR HAD FINALLY LEARNT TO STAND ON HIS OWN FOUR HOOVES ... **WITH A LITTLE HELP FROM HIS BIG SISTER!**

**THE END**

# Oat So Beautiful

Hello! Pinkie Pie here! Everypony deserves a little bit of pamper time now and again. Whenever I have a spare moment I love to make this all-natural facemask. It makes my skin feel super-duper soft and glowy so I'm ready for some serious party FUN ...

1. Mash the banana with a fork – a few lumps are fine!
2. Add in the oats and honey. Give the mixture a good stir.
3. Ask a grown-up or a friend to help you spread a layer of the mask on your face. It's best to stand over the sink when you do this.
4. Leave the mask on for about half an hour. I like to use this time to have a little Pinkie Pie pre-party snooze! Finally wash the mask off with warm water and gently pat your face dry.

## INGREDIENTS:

**(Makes enough for two masks, one for you and one for a friend.)**

Two tablespoons of oats

Half a ripe banana

One teaspoon of honey

## TOP TIPS:

Ask a grown-up before you make this mask.

The mask is a bit gloopy so put an old towel around your shoulders before you put it on your face.

# BADDIES, VILLAINS AND MEANIES

Do you think everypony in Equestria is nice? Think again! Here's Rainbow Dash's guide to who – or what – you should stay away from ...

## CRAGADILE

If there's one good reason **NOT** to go creeping around the Everfree Forest, this guy is it. Stronger than a crocodile and made of stone, it's one cranky creek-dweller!

## CERBERUS

This **GINORMOUS** three-headed beast guards a spooky city called Tartarus. I'd rather stick a super-sticky, icky strawberry-and-peppermint cupcake on my head than bump into this demon dog!

## LORD TIREK

Eeek! Take a look at this guy. He's super scary! This mixed-up centaur tries to steal the magic of others and even destroyed Twilight's former home, the Golden Oak Library. **NOT** nice!

## TATZLWURM

Eurgh! It took the combined magic of Twilight and Cadance to fight off this wriggling monster. Tatzlwurm lives deep underground but who knows when he'll raise his ugly head again!

## HYDRA

Wow – I thought that three heads were bad but this sickening serpent has FOUR. This smelly creature lives in a lonely swamp called Froggy Bottom Bogg. I suggest you stay away!

# Fluttershy's Favourite Fruity Scones

Well, hello there, friend! I love to bake for my animal pals and they all adore these delicious fruity treats – even fussy Angel Bunny. I like to eat my scones warm with a little jam and whipped cream. Yum!

## INGREDIENTS:

220g self-raising flour

50g butter at room temperature

20g white caster sugar

150ml milk

A handful of blueberries (cut the big ones in half)

1 beaten egg, for glazing

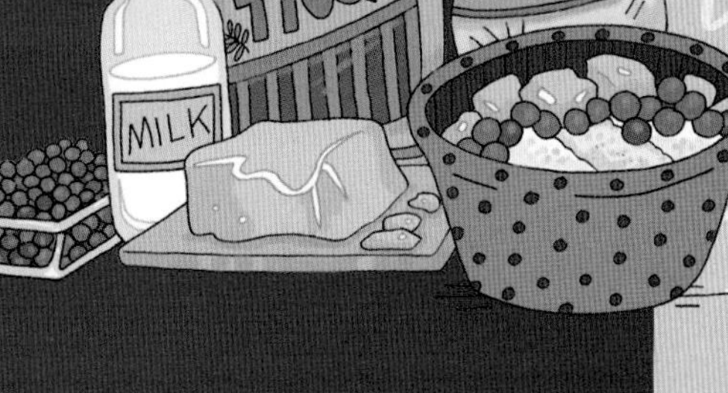


## YOU WILL NEED:

A helpful grown-up!

A large bowl

A rolling pin

A round pastry-cutter

A baking tray

A little extra flour for dusting

1

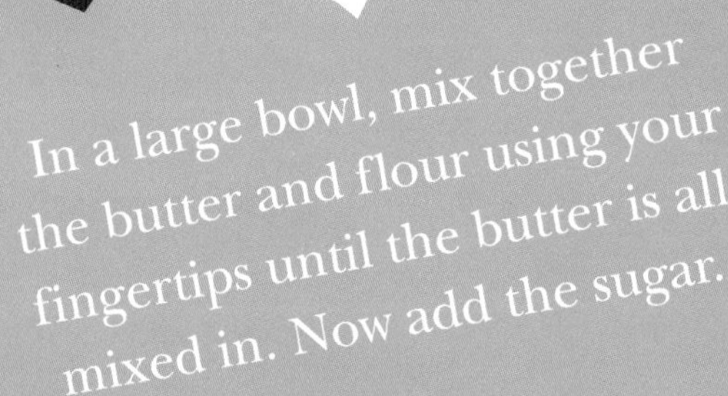

In a large bowl, mix together the butter and flour using your fingertips until the butter is all mixed in. Now add the sugar.

2

Next add the blueberries. Coating them in the flour mixture will help the fruit to keep its shape without popping in the oven.

**3**

Add ⅔ of the milk and mix very gently with a wooden spoon. If the mixture looks very dry, add some more milk – you should end up with a nice floury lump in the middle of the bowl.

**4**

Tip your scone mixture on to a floured worktop and knead together for a few seconds until it forms a round shape. Roll gently with the rolling pin until you reach a thickness of about 4 cm.

**5**

Using your favourite round cutter, cut as many circles from the dough as you can.

**6**

Place the circles on to your baking tray, at least 5 cm apart. Use your fingertips or a pastry brush to coat the tops of your scones with the egg wash – this will make your scones shiny.

**7**

Bake for about 15 minutes. The baked scones should be golden and bursting with delicious blueberries! Leave to cool for a few minutes before serving with jam and cream.

# What's Your Dream Job?

Each of the My Little Ponies is lucky enough to have a job that they love. But what would be your dream job? Take this special quiz to find out!

**1**

**What's your favourite subject at school?**

**A** English

**B** Sport

**C** Drama

**D** Science

**2**

**What do you like to do on a Saturday morning?**

**A** Read a book or buy a new magazine

**B** Go for a run or play a sport

**C** Work on a craft project or design a costume

**D** Play with your beloved pet!

**3**

**Your favourite possession is ...**

**A** Your notebook full of your thoughts and ideas

**B** Your trampoline

**C** Your dressing-up box

**D** Your brilliant collection of animal posters

4

**Which of these sounds most awesome?**

A Choosing new books for the school library

B Being made captain of your sports team

C Getting the lead in the school play

D Teaching your pet a brilliant new trick

5

**Your best ever treat would be ...**

A Meeting the author of your favourite book

B Winning tickets to the Olympic Games

C Going to see a brilliant play at the theatre

D Going for a horse ride on the beach

6

**Your friends describe you as ...**

A Creative and funny

B Energetic and a leader

C Smart and dramatic

D Kind and patient

## MOSTLY A'S

Your dream job is ...
**an author!**

You love reading and are full of ideas. Make sure you write down your dreams and thoughts – you never know when inspiration for a story might strike!

## MOSTLY B'S

Your dream job is ...
**an athlete!**

You are full of energy and love playing sports. Try lots of different sports and activities – you are sure to find one you truly love!

## MOSTLY C'S

Your dream job is ...
**an actress!**

You adore being the centre of attention and making people laugh. Why not try joining a local drama club, or putting on shows at home for your family?

## MOSTLY D'S

Your dream job is ... **a vet!**

You love animals more than anything. Veterinarians spend a lot of time learning how to do their job, so make sure you study hard and carry on having fun with your animal friends.

# Princess Celestia's WORDS OF WISDOM

The wonderful ruler of Equestria is full of knowledge and wisdom. Here she shares some very important life lessons with you ...

Be proud of what you do – but don't let that pride take over too much!

**Learning to trust your own instincts is one of the most valuable lessons to learn!**

SOMETIMES, THE SOLUTION TO YOUR PROBLEMS CAN COME FROM WHERE YOU LEAST EXPECT IT. ALWAYS LISTEN TO YOUR FRIENDS' OPINIONS AND IDEAS!

No matter where you go in life, never forget where you came from: your home, family and friends.

Never jump to conclusions – if you aren't sure about something, just ask.

**Being afraid can stop you from doing things that you love. But hiding behind these fears means you're hiding from your true self. Face your fears and you'll learn to overcome them!**

# Farewell, Friends!

Your pony friends have loved spending this time with you! Here are some very personal messages, just for you.

**TWILIGHT SPARKLE**

Listen to your heart and know that the magic of friendship is all around.

**RAINBOW DASH**

Never give up – keep true to your dreams and you'll make them come true!

**FLUTTERSHY**

Trust your instincts and be kind to everyone.

**RARITY**

Challenge yourself and remember you can always learn lessons from those around you.

**APPLEJACK**

Work hard – but accept that sometimes even YOU need a rest and change of scene!

**PINKIE PIE**

Sometimes you just need a break, a laugh or a scrumptious treat. Enjoy yourself and keep smiling!

# Answers

## WONDERBOLTS WORDSEARCH

| | | | | | | | | | |
|---|---|---|---|---|---|---|---|---|---|
| k | a | y | l | f | y | t | s | i | m |
| z | b | l | x | t | w | l | l | y | s |
| e | k | l | p | w | u | t | i | w | s |
| i | l | s | a | p | p | o | n | x | p |
| t | g | y | y | z | l | w | l | u | i |
| r | v | l | z | l | e | s | k | r | t |
| l | j | w | q | w | a | s | y | s | f |
| f | l | e | e | t | f | o | o | t | i |
| u | e | s | i | h | q | a | r | h | r |
| s | i | p | q | e | j | r | n | k | e |
| a | z | y | l | k | c | i | m | v | z |
| h | i | g | h | w | i | n | d | s | o |

## EYES ON THE PRIZE

## FAMILY FUN FOR EVERYONE

**1B, 2C, 3D, 4A, 5B, 6B, 7A, 8C.**

## CUTIE MARK CRAZINESS

## AHOY THERE, PIRATE PALS!

**Captain Celaeno** wears a large feather in her hat.

**Pirate Boyle** has just one hand.

**Pirate LixSpittle** carries cutlery in his pocket.

**Pirate Murdoch** always wears his goggles.

## PIRATE PONIES TO THE RESCUE

**These twelve things are different in picture two: Applejack:** (1) The apple is missing from her hat, (2) Her sword has changed colour. **Fluttershy:** (3) Angel Bunny's bandana is a different colour, (4) One stripe on Fluttershy's headband is a different colour. **Pinkie Pie:** (5) The spots on Pinkie's bandana are a different colour, (6) A gold button is missing from the front of her outfit. **Rarity:** (7) One diamond is missing from her hat, (8) Two of her legwarmers are a different colour. **Rainbow Dash:** (9) One of her legwarmers has changed colour, (10) A ring is missing from her wing. **Princess TS:** (11) Two stars are missing from her hat, (12) One legwarmer is a different colour.

## A MISSION FOR TEMPEST

## CODE CRACKERS

**DREAMS ARE FOR EVERYPONY**

## UNDERWATER I-SPY

**(1) A jellyfish (2) Purple (3) Shells (4) A tail (5) Orange**

## STORY TIME

**Friendship, magic, help, gems, apple, bird, clouds, balloon, Songbird, cake, Equestria**

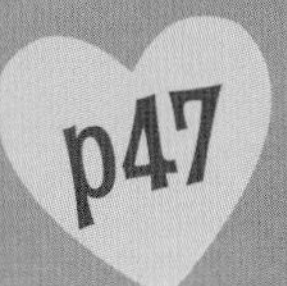

## GUESS WHO?

**1: Flurry Heart; 2: Rainbow Dash; 3: Spike; 4: Pinkie Pie**

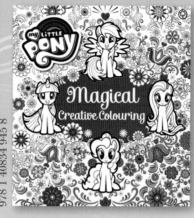

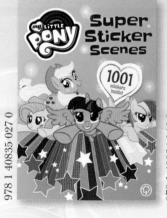

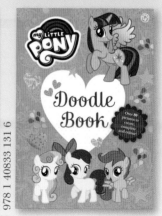

# Spellbinding Stories from My Little Pony!

978 1 40833 123 1

978 1 40833 121 7

978 1 40833 122 4

978 1 40834 468 2

978 1 40833 704 2

978 1 40833 695 3

978 1 40833 702 8

978 1 40833 833 9

978 1 40834 476 7

978 1 40833 831 5

978 1 40834 149 0

978 1 40834 466 8

ORCHARD